Storytime Stickers

Santa's On His Way

By Mark Shulman

Illustrated by Kathy Wilburn

Sterling Publishing Co., Inc.
New York

2 4 6 8 10 9 7 5 3 1

Published by Sterling Publishing Co., Inc.
387 Park Avenue South, New York, NY 10016
Text © 2006 by Mark Shulman
Illustrations © 2006 by Kathy Wilburn
Distributed in Canada by Sterling Publishing
c/o Canadian Manda Group, 165 Dufferin Street,
Toronto, Ontario, Canada M6K 3H6
Distributed in the United Kingdom by GMC Distribution Services,
Castle Place, 166 High Street, Lewes, East Sussex, England BN7 1XU
Distributed in Australia by Capricorn Link (Australia) Pty. Ltd.
P.O. Box 704, Windsor, NSW 2756, Australia

Printed in China
All rights reserved

Sterling ISBN-13: 978-1-4027-3585-1
ISBN-10: 1-4027-3585-5

For information about custom editions, special sales, premium and
corporate purchases, please contact Sterling Special Sales
Department at 800-805-5489 or specialsales@sterlingpub.com.

Every year around December
there's a place that's full of life.
If you get a chance to spy it,
you'll find Santa and his wife.

See the busy elves all working,
making games and dolls and toys.
What they're building is excitement
for a world of girls and boys.

Santa works inside his office
reading children's lists of hope,
checking out who's nice and naughty
through his special telescope.

**Find the reindeer getting ready
on December twenty-fourth—
sleeping, checking maps, and playing
in their hideaway up north.**

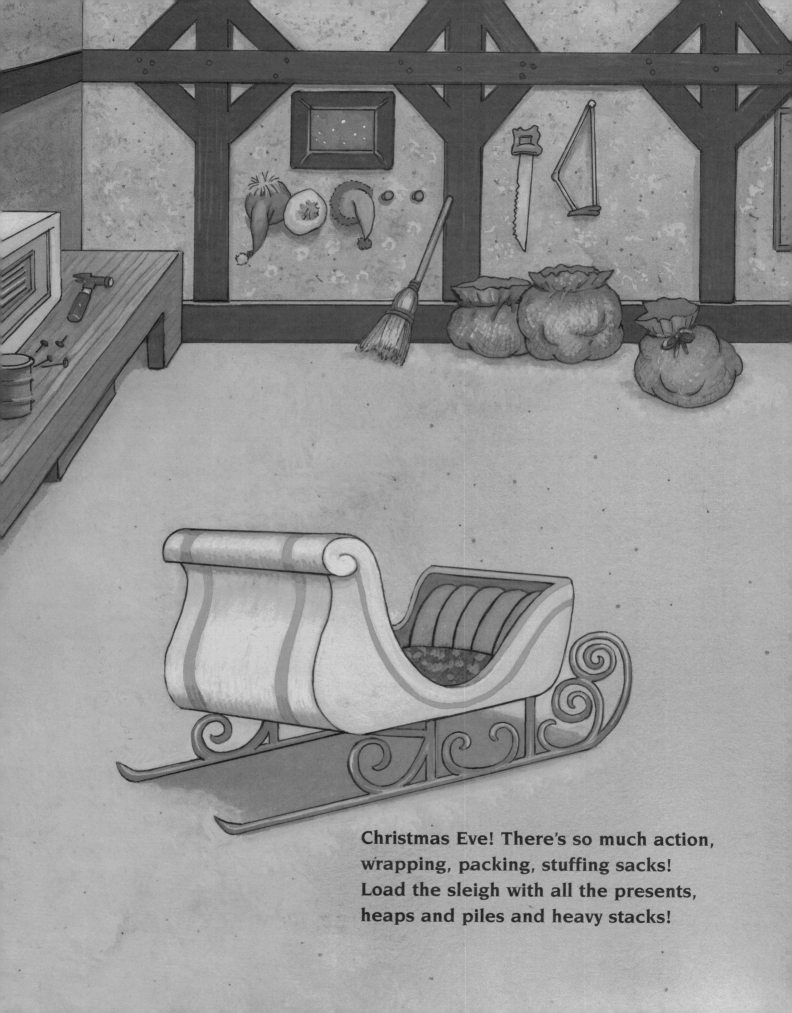

Christmas Eve! There's so much action,
wrapping, packing, stuffing sacks!
Load the sleigh with all the presents,
heaps and piles and heavy stacks!

In the inky dark they're flying.
Reindeer pull the mighty sleigh.
Santa Claus prepares for landing.
Christmas Eve is under way!

Land the reindeer! Eat the cookies!
Leave the presents! Hide and peek!
Christmastime is very busy.
Where will Santa be next week?

The sand is warm, the water's clear.
See you in another year!